the Whedonite

ARIA GLAZKI

ANIKA PRESS

Every time somebody opens their mouth they have an opportunity to do one of two things—connect or divide.

— Joss Whedon

One

"OH FOR CRYING OUT LOUD." Mira dropped the bags cutting into her fingers so she could smack the door. Her key protruded from the lock at a broken angle. She flicked the dangling *Doctor Horrible* goggles then smacked the door again. Because that would definitely help.

"You all right there?"

"Oh! Uh." Mira glanced at the guy who'd spoken then surveyed the mass of shopping bags that were now blocking the entire hallway. "Sorry!" Her fingers found the dratted key, tugging and twisting futilely. "It gets stuck sometimes. Just two minutes. Or, you know, here." She stopped fiddling with the key to try and corral her mess so he could pass. "Sorry."

A quizzical smile met her babbling. His gaze stilled on her head, reminding Mira of the Jayne hat she still wore. She must look like such a spaz! Which was a shame, since this guy was kind of cute, with his tousled hair and rectangular, black-rimmed glasses. "Sorry," she repeated idiotically, tugging the hat off. At least her unruly curly hair was contained today in a ponytail.

His gaze fell to the mound of plastic bags. "Are you having a party?"

"A Whedon night, at the store I manage. Sorry." She tried gathering the bags again. "Are you visiting someone?" she asked

1

casually, hoping to mask the flush of red burning up her cheeks. She definitely hadn't seen him here before, though to be fair, she didn't know most of the people in her building.

He leaned down, helping her stuff spilled items back into the plastic then picking up a couple of bags. "I'm subletting, actually, from one of your neighbors."

"Oh." Mira nodded when they both straightened. "Uh, well. Welcome to the building."

"Thanks." Her new neighbor cleared his throat, flooding Mira with a fresh wave of embarrassment.

"Sorry." She reached for the bags in his hands, but his chin tilted toward her door.

"Your key."

"Right! Oh. Sorry." Mira's fingers found the traitorous bit of metal, biting back some expletives as she jiggled it free of the lock and reinserted it properly. Finally, the tumbler clicked, releasing the handle. She dumped the bags she held inside, murmuring a quick *thanks* when he held out the rest.

Silence stretched between them. Was it too late to ask his name? He'd probably prefer she just got out of his way. "So, um."

"Yeah." His shoulders lifted as his hands found his pockets. "Hey, uh. What's a Whedon?"

"One of three overly talented brothers." Her quip was met with lowered eyebrows. "Sorry. Joss Whedon, he's a writer. Well, and a director, and producer. He created *Firefly*, *Buffy*, *Angel*, *Dollhouse*, and directed that Avengers movie that came out recently, which then spawned *Agents of S.H.I.E.L.D.* He's kind of brilliant. I mean, his characters are just so whole, and complex, and richly layered. And he has these plot lines that entirely subvert expectations, but without any ridiculous leaps or plot holes. Plus layered in everything are these insightful, and occasionally terrifying, social commentaries…" She trailed off. "Sorry." She really had to stop babbling. Most people would have made some excuse to get away from her by now, but he was somewhat trapped by the small hallway.

"No, it's cool. I take it you're a fan."

"In a world of the streamlined, superficial, over-processed mindlessness that passes for entertainment nowadays, he kind of stands out. Which tends to congregate other incredibly talented people around him, and that in turn means the creation of some pretty unique and thought-provoking, yet deeply emotive stories."

His eyes widened behind his glasses. "Gotcha. Sounds interesting."

"Sorry. Didn't mean to talk your ear off."

"No, no. It's nice, actually. I don't know too many people here yet." His lips lengthened into a gently curving smile, melting something in her insides.

"Oh, well, you should come! To the store's Whedon Night, I mean. On the twenty-third."

"Okay. Thanks. Guess I'll—" A ringtone cut him off. He slipped out his phone, quieting the tone, then looked back to Mira, shrugging slightly.

"I'll let you grab that," Mira said, a little disappointed.

"Yeah, I should. Guess I'll see you around."

She waved at him lamely, and he made his way down the hall to the end unit. Mira stepped inside her apartment and kicked the bags out of the way so she could shut the door. She leaned against it and sighed. *Such a spaz.*

Jordan opened the refrigerator for the fourth time, as if something suitable for dinner would have magically appeared in the last ten minutes. A bag of bagels, a tub of cream cheese, and a carton of orange juice from a nearby Bruegger's stared back at him. He really needed to find a grocery store at some point. So far, he'd mostly been living on takeout from the Chinese place on the corner, and the bagels.

He let the door drift shut yet again. There had to be a better option for dinner. He wouldn't have minded going out, but he didn't really know anybody here other than his coworkers, and to be honest, he saw enough of them during the day.

There was that girl he'd bumped into—one of his new neighbors. She was a little weird, and way too into those TV shows she'd talked about, but maybe she'd be up for dinner. It'd beat eating alone at any rate. And some of the things she'd said sounded smart, not just blindly fanatic, so there was that.

Besides, it was one meal. The worst thing that could happen was it'd be boring, and then they'd see each other every so often in the halls. Awkward, but manageable, unless she was that obsessive about everything in her life.

He plopped back onto the couch, reaching for his computer. Maybe he should just find a new delivery place to try.

Or he could give this a shot, getting to know her. She was a head shorter than him, so he could probably handle it if she did go full-blown crazy.

Jordan glanced again at the bare room, then shut his laptop and headed for the door. How bad could one dinner be?

He didn't hesitate again until right after knocking. Trying the adult equivalent of ding-dong-ditch crossed his mind, but the door opened to reveal his neighbor. Jordan's gaze fell to the purple stripe in her dark, curly hair before finding her almond eyes. She was actually sort of pretty, in a quirky way. "Uh, hey," he got out before seeing the two other women in the apartment behind her.

"Hi."

"I'm Jordan, by the way, I don't think we actually introduced ourselves the other day."

"Mira," she said with a blank smile. This was going well.

"Sorry, I didn't realize you had company." Idiotically, the possibility hadn't even crossed his mind.

"Oh!" She glanced over her shoulder as if she'd forgotten her friends were there. "Uh, yeah. Is everything okay?"

"Yeah, of course." Though inviting her to dinner wasn't an option now, which left him standing in her doorway for no reason.

Mira's eyebrows crooked as she waited for him to say something.

"Ah, you know…" Now would be a good time for his brain to kick in. "I was just wondering if you knew any good restaurants around, for takeout or delivery."

"Oh sure, sorry. Yeah. What kind of food do you like?"

One of the other women—a blonde with glasses—cleared her throat.

"Uh, right." Mira's cheeks grew pink. "Or, you could join us? We were planning on ordering in."

"No, no. I wouldn't want to intrude."

"No, please," her other friend said.

"You wouldn't be," Mira assured. "If you're up for our company, that is."

Well, it did solve the problem of eating alone. "If you're sure," Jordan said, giving them another chance to get rid of him.

"We're sure!" the blonde called.

Mira chuckled then stepped back, gesturing silently for him to come in.

Jordan didn't look entirely uncomfortable, even if they had basically shanghaied him into joining them for dinner. Mira considered the piles of supplies covering her couch and coffee table. The plan had been to spend the night making various gift packs and prizes for the party. That definitely wasn't going to help her make a more normal second impression.

"So." She shut the door, scrambling for a topic. Jordan watched her intently. "Sorry, uh, that's Lisa and Kelsey."

"Nice to meet you," Jordan said, nodding at no one in particular.

"So we were thinking Thai for dinner," Lisa jumped in. Mira exhaled. Lisa was way better with the whole socializing thing. "Or Italian. Or technically, we could do both."

"Weird palate mix," Kelsey said, scrunching her nose. "But you know," she backtracked, looking at Jordan, "whatever you want."

"No, hey. I'm interrupting your evening. I'm up for anything."

"Ooh la la," Lisa teased with a flirty smile.

Jordan froze for a second, then laughed, instantly put at ease.

Mira stuffed down the pang of jealousy. Her own faltering attempts at flirting usually involved stammering, blushing, and scaring people off. Not that she wanted to flirt with Jordan; it would just be nice to have that kind of effortlessness. "Please, make yourself comfortable," she murmured as the dutiful host.

He glanced her way with a *thanks* before joining Lisa on a newly cleared spot on the couch.

"So, Italian?" Kelsey asked, bringing over the menu from La Gondola. "Personally, I'm craving some cheesy goodness."

"So where do you rank on the Whedonite scale?" the blonde—*Lisa*—asked with a smile after they'd ordered the food.

Jordan took in the miscellany of items in the living room, from a wooden box, to a pile of button-making supplies on a stack of pictures of a hammer, to three of those orange-and-yellow, knit hats like the one Mira had worn when they'd met. "Well, Mira just told me about it the other day," he admitted.

"Oh. We're kind of obsessed," Lisa confided, glancing at the other women. "But I promise, other than that, we're pretty normal. Kelsey's even a mom."

Jordan looked to the slightly older brunette as she came out of the kitchen. "Oh yeah?"

"To two wonderful boys, who are spending tonight bonding with their daddy." She brought over a pitcher of iced tea, followed by Mira with some glasses. "What do you do, Jordan?"

"I'm a mechanical engineer. Thanks." He took the proffered glass she'd poured. "I just moved here from Denver, for work."

"Oh, very nice." Kelsey nodded with approval. "Lisa's working on her Ph.D. in engineering, over at Carnegie Mellon."

"Electrical, but yeah," the blonde confirmed.

"Cool, that's a great program." He turned back to Mira, who hadn't said much since he'd come in. "And you own a store?"

"Manage—a bookstore. That's what all this stuff is for. We run a different fan night a few times a year. Though this one is actually my favorite."

The other women murmured their agreement. Jordan searched his surroundings for something useful to say. "So what's up with the hammers?"

That set off a round of giggles.

"It's a superhero thing," Kelsey explained. "Captain Hammer."

"Have you seen any Whedon shows?" Lisa asked.

"Yeah, uh, *The Avengers*. You said that was one of his, right?"

"It is, yeah," Mira confirmed. "But there he was working with Marvel characters. Captain Hammer is one of his originals. It's actually a pretty cool story, if you remember the writer's strike from a few years back?"

"Sure, yeah." He didn't watch much TV anyway, but it had upset a bunch of people that new episodes of their shows were delayed.

Mira hesitated then shook her head, sending her curls flying a bit. "Sorry, I'm geeking out again."

"Basically," Lisa jumped in, "a bunch of talented people got together, decided they didn't need a major studio, and put out this mini movie-musical for free online. Plenty of satire, fun lyrics, good jokes. Most people don't even catch everything the first time around. Or really, the fifth time around, for some."

The women laughed again.

"You know, I haven't seen it in ages," Kelsey said.

"Oh, well, we could watch it tonight. I mean, if you're interested," Mira offered, looking at him.

Jordan smiled reflexively. "Sure." Their food hadn't arrived yet, and he was clearly outnumbered. Besides, the show might be good.

✧ ✧ ✧

"He seems nice," Kelsey said, helping Mira bring the dishes to the kitchen.

"Yes, he does."

"Cute, too."

Mira tried to fight the blush that loved frequenting her cheeks. "Don't you have a husband?"

"Doesn't make me blind."

"He seems to get along well with Lisa," Mira said as another swell of laughter reached them. It wasn't all that surprising really. Of the three women, Lisa probably had the most in common with him, simply by virtue of their career choices. Kelsey was an English lit. teacher, and Mira was far from a brainiac, especially when it came to STEM subjects.

"He didn't come here for Lisa," Kelsey pointed out kindly.

"No, he came here because he doesn't know anyone else in town. The spazzy geek two doors down was his only option." She pulled out a box of cookies in case someone wanted dessert. They hadn't even gotten started on making the things she needed for the store.

"Oh, come now. He probably saw a beautiful girl he wanted to get to know better. Who," Kelsey said pointedly when Mira was about to speak, "is passionate about something. That's not a bad thing."

"Maybe." There wasn't much use arguing with Kelsey. "And then he found Lisa, the smart, athletic, gorgeous blonde who's managed to talk to him about something other than Joss Whedon."

Kelsey's hand landed on hers. "He seemed to like *Doctor Horrible*."

"Well, who doesn't," Mira teased.

"Okay, fair enough. But I'm telling you, you shouldn't give up just like that. Lisa'd back off if she knew you liked him."

"I don't," Mira protested. "Sure, he's good looking, but I don't even know him. If he and Lisa want to get together, more power to them. I have my hands full with this party, anyway." Not that she'd mind having her hands full with some*one* instead of something.

Kelsey's lips twisted to the side as she shot Mira her disbelieving mom look. A second later, she scooped up the cookies and headed back to the living room. Mira exhaled, pasted on a fresh smile, and followed.

"So what's with the box?" Jordan asked as she settled back on one of her overstuffed chairs.

The impact of his gaze distracted Mira for a moment.

"A vampire-slaying kit," Lisa told him.

"If we ever get around to making one," Mira joked, then mentally kicked herself. There was a ton of work to do, but it wasn't like she wanted him to leave. Though she didn't exactly want to do all of the work on her own after everyone had gone, either.

"What does that entail?" Jordan asked.

"Wooden stakes, an axe, some holy water." Lisa managed to make even that list sound flirty. She'd tried giving Mira some tips once on a night out, but that had been almost more disastrous than Mira's own awkwardness.

"A cross, of course," Kelsey added.

"Garlic?" Jordan's eyebrows curved almost perfectly over his glasses.

"Not in the Buffy-verse," Mira said apologetically.

"You guys are going to make all that?"

"That's the plan," Kelsey confirmed, shifting to leadership mode. "Actually, we should really get started."

"Oh, well I should get out of your guys' way," Jordan said. "I mean, I'd be happy to help, but I'm not all that crafty."

Kelsey squinted, pretending to size him up. "I bet you could handle making buttons, while we do the hard stuff."

The three of them shared a laugh, already enviably comfortable around each other. Mira shook herself mentally and pushed out of her chair. "Right, sorry. Let me find us some scissors."

Jordan had to admit, the night had gone better than he'd thought it would. The food had been great, Mira's friends were funny, and they were all really creative. They'd made buttons, the slaying kit, a couple unique tee shirts, and materials for challenges they had planned, all in a few hours.

Mira herself was intelligent and nice, when she was talking to anyone but him. Maybe she hadn't appreciated him barging in on their night. Or, maybe she was just shy. Hopefully it was the latter. She did apologize a lot, but that was kind of cute.

Point was, he'd had fun tonight. It would be good to have some people to hang out with while he got his bearings, even if this didn't turn into any lasting friendships. At the very least, it looked like he had plans for the twenty-third.

Doctor Horrible's Sing-Along Blog had been unexpected and insightful. He'd even finally learned what an antihero was, which would make his high school English teachers happy. Plus, parts of the special feature with fan auditions for the Evil League of Evil had been hilarious. So maybe they were onto something, with this Whedon guy. He might even check out some of those other shows on Netflix.

Two

CAN I HELP YOU FIND YOUR NEXT READ?" Mira asked, walking toward the man standing by their "Blind Date with a Book" display.

He let the wrapped book in his hands drop back to the table. "Just figured I'd try your"—he turned toward her—"matchmaking services."

"Oh hi, Jordan." She brightened her professional smile despite the light flutter in her stomach.

His head tilted when he recognized her. "Mira. Is this your store?"

"Yep." So much for the possibility that he'd come to see her. "This is it. Are you looking for a mysterious read?"

"I guess, yeah." He glanced back at the display. "I was just passing by, saw your sign. Thought it could be a fairly failsafe option for a date."

"I doubt you have problems finding dates." *There you go, Mira. Be even more of a spaz.* "A good book, now, that can be hard to find."

"Well, maybe you could help me pick something out." His lips tugged up at the corners, feeding that ridiculous flutter.

"Of course. What are you in the mood for?"

"You know, I'm not sure."

"Okay, well, we have some staff recommendations." She pulled the ring of colorful, handwritten flash cards toward them. "Or, you could take a risk, pick a book at random from one of these. All of the descriptions are honest, so it won't say thriller and really be a romance or anything like that."

He nodded, flipping absently through the flash cards. Mira's eyes lingered on the blunt lines of his jaw, picking out the hint of a dimple. And man, did those glasses look good on him!

"Hey, Mira?"

She blinked herself off the entirely inappropriate train of thought to face Charlie, her newest hire. "What's up?"

"Could you help me with this return?" Charlie glanced over her shoulder toward an all-too-familiar older woman, who had a tendency to treat the store like her own private library.

"I'll be right there." Mira looked back to Jordan. "Excuse me a sec? I'm sorry."

"Of course, no problem." He flashed her a perfectly polite, and entirely indifferent, smile.

Mira turned away, puffing her breath out in the few steps toward the cash register, before pulling her lips into a fresh smile for Mrs. Castini. "How can I help you today?" she asked, starting their weekly dance.

Not long after, the store's bell chimed, and she caught a glimpse of Jordan leaving, book– and date–free.

The bookstore's bell chimed cheerfully as Jordan stepped back inside, but Mira wasn't out front. He chose one end of the store and strode up the aisle toward the back. It wouldn't take much time to see if she was elsewhere in the store, and worst-case scenario he'd take the pastries he'd gotten, pick a mystery "blind date" book, and head home, even if that did mean spending the afternoon alone.

Happily, he found her a few aisles over, beside a trolley piled with books. He debated for half a second before making his way to her side. "Hey."

Her head snapped toward him. "Hey, uh, hi. Sorry, I thought you'd left."

He held up the white paper bag. "Thought I might have a better chance of convincing you to take a break if I came with pastries."

Her lips parted before she exhaled with a small smile. "That's, wow, that's very nice of you. But I really can't take a break right now, I'm sorry."

Either she was genuinely disappointed or Jordan was about to cross the line to creepiness, but he really didn't want to go back to his empty apartment. "Well, maybe I could help?" Offering had worked last time, at least.

"You want to help me stock shelves?"

"Sure. It's authors' last names, right? I think I remember the alphabet."

Mira chuckled, looking down as her cheeks turned pink. "Okay, um, thanks." She took another book and turned toward the shelf.

Jordan smiled, setting the pastries on an unoccupied part of the trolley, and picked up a couple books, then turned them to see the spines.

"So did you always want to be an engineer?" Mira asked a few seconds later. "Were you on the robotics team in high school and all that?"

"Well, no, actually, not at all."

"Oh." She glanced briefly up at him before picking up more books and moving a few steps away. "Sorry."

"No, it's just, I mostly played sports in high school. That kept me pretty busy, and I didn't think about the long-term much. Then a friend got me to go to a robotics competition, one time senior year, and I just realized how cool it was. I mean, building your own robot that actually functions, that can do anything, you know? So I decided I wanted to do that, and that meant studying engineering. And well, here I am now, a full-fledged geek."

"I don't think you can say that if you're not part of at least three fandoms." She shot him a smile over her shoulder.

"Oh yeah? Must have missed that rule in my copy of the geek handbook."

"Sorry, but it's true. Three fandoms or at least one obsession with an alternate reality RPG."

The snappy witticism distracted him momentarily from the books, and he could outright feel his cheeks tighten into a grin. "So what about you? What brought you into bookstore management?"

Mira stepped around him in the aisle to reach for more books. He wasn't actually doing that great a job helping her, but she didn't seem to mind. Jordan picked up another book anyway.

"I was never really good at anything besides reading, so I've worked in bookstores and libraries for pretty much every job I ever had, except one generally disastrous attempt at being an office assistant. Plus, someone has to help keep indie bookstores alive."

"Alive? What do you mean?"

Mira stopped working to actually look at him. "You know, with independent bookstores closing, going bankrupt, all over the country, actually probably the world. I mean, if titans like Borders can't stay open, where does that leave us?" She turned away, refocusing on her work, but Jordan just watched her talk. "Between digital publishing, online distributors, and publishers wanting to make more money while readers want to pay less, we're all barely hanging on. Even when we can offer the same prices as, say, Amazon, the fact that they offer free shipping means most people will order a book directly to their door rather than going to the effort of coming into a store. It's why we now stock certain movies, and comic books, of course. The simple pleasure of holding a well-crafted, beautifully bound book is considered by most a thing of the past." She turned back to him then seemed to remember that she was supposed to be shy. "Sorry."

"You apologize a lot."

She broke eye contact, looking down yet again. "Yeah, sorry."

"No, that's—you don't have to apologize." He grabbed another book to break the awkwardness. "I didn't know that, about bookstores being in such dire straits. I wonder if there's a gimmick of some kind, something that would draw people here without seeming like a marketing scheme."

"You mean, besides hosting parties like next weekend's, and basically stalking authors online to convince them to do events here, or at the very least come sign some books?"

It was amazing, the way she switched between timidity and self-assurance. "Right, of course. I meant…something differ-ent, I guess." And how her confidence made him tongue-tied.

"I'm happy to hear ideas if you have some," she said earnestly, her smile rounding her cheeks.

"Maybe a mascot?"

"Like…a talking book?"

"Huh, no. Maybe not. That could get a little creepy." A reading robot could be cool, though, and a fun project too.

Mira laughed outright, picking up the final few books on the cart. "This is why they pay me the exceedingly mediocre bucks."

"Well." Jordan grabbed the bag he'd brought, silently mulling over the feasibility of his idea. "Even more reason for you to take a break."

Three

MAN, I LOVE YOUR EYES," Lisa murmured while staring at Mira, checking her handiwork.

"They're too far apart," Mira said, trying not to move.

Lisa sat back, letting Mira see more than her friend's nose. "You're kidding, right? They're slightly wide-set, but that's part of makes you so gorgeous. And it's totally in."

"Whatever you say." Mira had no illusions about her looks. Her face was too round, her eyes too far apart, her hair way too unmanageable, and she was crazy short, and a bit plump. It wasn't a great combination. "So, are you done trying to work a miracle on me? There's only so much even you can do," Mira teased. Lisa was amazing with makeup, especially when it came to cosplay.

"Come here," she said, leaning forward and picking up another brush. A couple swipes over Mira's eyebrows, and she was officially proclaimed done.

"Great, thank you." Mira looked in the mirror, a tiny, secret part of her hoping she'd been transformed into someone pretty. She blinked away the disappointment. "You're amazing, as you know. But we're running low on time, and I still have to figure out what to do with my hair."

In the reflection, Lisa's eyebrows lowered. "I thought you already did it."

Mira sighed. "I don't know about leaving it down."

"Well, you should, because it looks fabulous. And Inara wears hers like that all the time. With your dress on, you'll look perfect."

"You think so?" Mira twisted toward the outfit on her bed. She'd splurged recently to have the dress made, exactly like one of Inara's. It was sleeveless and a shimmery purple, with a golden accent spilling from a slit in the front and a deep vee neckline that showcased her bust, which was arguably Mira's best physical asset. The coolest part of the dress was the cut of the skirt, which hid the jiggly part of her stomach, even with the golden belt. A golden cuff and a matching necklace-and-earring set completed the look.

"I know so." Lisa plopped onto the bed, ready to go in her Harmony costume, which basically consisted of dressing up like a somewhat slutty bombshell and pretending to be vapid. Lisa had also ditched her glasses and added a fake trickle of blood from the corner of her mouth. "So get dressed already," she instructed with a smile.

It didn't take long to pull on all the pieces. Mira glanced back at the mirror before slipping on her shoes. She actually looked okay, though goodness knew how long that would last. They'd already cleared the temporary displays from the front of the store, to replace them with tables, but they still needed to set up the refreshments, prizes, and contest supplies. And she'd be running around like crazy most of the night, which also meant having to forego heels. Then again, it wasn't like people would be there to look at her. Still, it was too bad the outfit wouldn't endow her with Inara's confidence and poise.

Chatter from the bookstore encased him the moment Jordan opened the door, entirely at odds with the near silence of his last visit. A couple dozen strangers in a bizarre array of costumes were clumped in smaller groups around tables that had replaced the previous book displays. Animated conversations and bursts of laughter put the point on just how far out of his element Jordan was. He almost turned around to leave when a familiar face came into view.

"Jordan!" Mira's friend Kelsey instantly handed him one of the Captain Hammer buttons they'd made. "Glad you're here. There's a coat rack in the back if you'd like, and the various activities will start up pretty soon. Oh, there's no need for that." She waved away the ten-dollar bill he'd dug out of his pocket. "You're on the list," she added with a wink.

"Thanks," Jordan managed to get out as she ushered him toward the back. He made a mental note to buy a few more books, too, to make up for it.

The back of the store was much quieter, with the books buffering the bustle of the front. Jordan shrugged off his jacket and added it to the sparsely populated coatrack. This was just a party, not an interview or a test.

After a few deep breaths, he headed back toward the refreshment table—as safe a place to start as any—then slowed when one of the groups split up, exposing Mira. She had her hair down today and wore a sexy purple dress, and the smile she shot the couple walking away was beautiful. "You look great," he told her, stepping up toward the table where she was resettling the platters.

Her smile dropped as she turned toward him, then her lips shifted into a shyer curve. "Thanks." Her eyes dipped down his torso before she met his gaze again with a more distant, if brighter, smile. "And you, you make a great Doctor Tam."

Temporarily confused, Jordan glanced down at the vest he wore over a simple white shirt. "Oh, yeah. Well, I actually just wore what your friends told me to," he admitted.

"Right, of course. So then, they made a great choice."

"Well, I can't take any credit. But you really do look fantastic."

Her smile slipped back to the cute, shy version for half a second before her chin ducked, and she refocused on fidgeting with the table, moving a dish of crackers a millimeter to the left and a bowl of chips half an inch closer to the edge. Jordan searched for something else to say, but they had yet to talk much about anything other than Joss Whedon and the fate of independent bookstores. Asking how their sales were doing seemed a little inappropriate.

For better or worse, they were joined by a couple of others at the table. One guy wore a long, brown coat, and the other looked like he was pretty much wearing normal clothes except for an eye patch. Like Jordan's own "costume," they could easily have passed for absolutely normal on the street. For that matter, maybe they weren't actually wearing costumes.

"Nice Simon Tam, dude," the guy with the eye patch said by way of greeting.

"And you got your girlfriend to dress up, too," the brown-coated guy said, giving Mira a once-over. "That's awesome, man. My girl wouldn't even consider coming to one of these, forget dressing like a companion."

"That's unfortunate. Maybe if you introduced her to some more characters in the Whedonverse, she'd change her mind," Mira suggested.

Brown Coat scoffed. "Nah, she has more in her life than pleasing her man. She doesn't need to beg for attention by pretending she understands the stuff I'm into. Unlike *some*," he added with a smirk.

Eye Patch sniggered.

"Hey, enough." Jordan stepped slightly between them and Mira.

"C'mon, man," Brown Coat said, gesturing dismissively with a cube of cheese. "She's the one dressed as a companion."

"Oh, geeze, I know," Eye Patch chimed in, turning to Mira. "Do you even know the name of the character you're dressed as?"

"Amazingly, you seem to have misunderstood pretty much every point Whedon was trying to make with Inara, and with companions," Mira said calmly. "Which is really rather impressive, in a way, having such an impenetrable skull protecting the unused mass that serves as your brain."

Jordan bit back a laugh, but the two guys merely exchanged confused looks as the insult sailed past them.

"You're dressed like a whore," Brown Coat eventually said.

"And you're not even pretty enough to be one," Eye Patch instantly added.

"Don't talk to her like that." Jordan said, turning squarely toward the two other men. "Apologize to her. And then you should leave."

Brown Coat scoffed, crossing his arms over his chest. "We don't have to go anywhere, or apologize. To anyone. The character she's dressed as *is* a whore."

"Actually," Mira said, drawing all of their attention, "Whedonverse misconceptions aside, this is a private estalishment, and as such, we have exclusive control over the attendees of our private events. So you do have to leave."

"Whatever. You know what, if you work here, we want to talk to your manager," Eye Patch said, mimicking Brown Coat's pose. "And our money back."

"I am the manager," Mira said, still amazingly calm. "But I'll gladly refund your money on your way out." She gestured for them to precede her to the door.

The two idiots looked disbelievingly at Jordan, as if it was still his word that mattered.

"Was I unclear?" Mira said firmly.

The guys exchanged glances then, still huffing, turned toward the door.

"Hey, Mira, I'm sorry. That wasn't okay," Jordan said when they were out of earshot.

Mira glanced at him over her shoulder. "Don't be. None of that was your fault." Her expression softened with a small smile. "Thanks, for standing up to them."

"Yeah. Sure," he said to her back. He watched her walk to the store's entrance then turned to the refreshment table to occupy his hands, though maybe he should have followed them out, so he didn't cause her to lose any more business.

"Look who I found," he heard a few seconds later.

"Hi, Lisa." Should he tell her about the red stain by her mouth? Then again it might be intentional, like the other weird details he'd noticed in people's outfits.

"Don't you look dapper, if a bit confused." She swiped a small cluster of grapes from the table. "Don't worry, the trivia challenge will start up soon, and then you'll see that most of us in this room don't know as much about Joss Whedon as we like to pretend we do, especially now that his work includes both the Marvel universe and Shakespeare."

"There were like ten things there I didn't understand, so we're right on track," Jordan teased.

Lisa laughed comfortably, glancing around them at the store. "So what's new?" she asked, looking back to him.

"Well, actually, since it's just us. You're studying EE, right?"

She hummed her confirmation, eyes widening curiously.

This might be a horrible idea, but she could always turn him down. There was no harm in asking, right? "I was hoping, well, maybe I could get your help with something, a little project I'm working on."

"Okay, last song guys," Mira called to the group of college kids singing "I've Got a Theory" from *Once More With Feeling*.

A chorus of halfhearted boos met the statement.

"How 'bout a ten-dollar solo?" one guy dressed as an Initiative soldier called, waving the named bill.

"Yeah, c'mon, just a couple more," pleaded the girl hanging off of him, who was dressed in a much sexier bunny suit than Anya's had ever been.

"Okay, all right," Mira relented. They were having fun, and she had plenty of cleaning up to do. "A couple more."

The small group cheered, and Mira smiled, dumping a bowl of leftover chips into a plastic bag.

Overall, it seemed the night could be called a success, though she had yet to tally the receipts. The trivia competition had had decent participation, with Kelsey's oldest son surprising everyone with his knowledge. Of course, the harder questions had knocked him out of the running, but that was true for almost all of the participants, as was the point. People had started leaving soon after the costume contest's results had been announced, with first place going to a truly impressive cosplay of Lorne. Now there were only the college kids, a few lingerers enjoying their off-key serenades, plus a couple more people browsing the shelves.

As the guy jumped in on his girlfriend's "ten-dollar solo," Mira brought the leftovers to her office then headed for the register to cash out. Maybe their next Whedon event should involve a live performance of *Doctor Horrible*, backed by the movie, sort of in the vein of *Rocky Horror* shows. That would only take four major performers, and the rest could be sung by the audience, really making it a sing-along. She'd have to run the idea past her friends, to see if it was completely nuts, but it could be fun.

"Trifecta, huh?" Jordan asked, coming up to the register.

Mira's gaze jumped to his face. They hadn't interacted much since she'd kicked out the two jerks from earlier, though she'd kept getting distracted by glimpses of him among the other guests. Things had gotten so hectic toward the end, she hadn't realized he had stuck around.

"Is it really that good?" he asked, nodding to their *Much Ado About Nothing* display.

"The play?" Mira asked stupidly. She'd decided to offer bundle pricing on copies of the original play, the 1993 movie, and of course, Joss Whedon's recent take. A few bundles had even sold.

"Well yeah, and the movies." His lips lengthened into a smile. "Let me guess," he said, tapping a DVD of Whedon's movie, "this one's your favorite."

Mira chuckled, straightening their bookmark display to avoid getting pulled in by Jordan's friendly gaze. "Um, no. I don't know, actually," she finally answered. "The Kenneth Branagh version is pretty fantastic, traditional. Of course Whedon's version is entirely different, his interpretation and the modern setting, even though he kept Shakespeare's language. And the actors in each are undeniably talented. I don't know that I'd say either version is better than the other. Sorry."

"This is just a sales ploy isn't it?" He leaned his elbows on the counter in front of her, bringing the two of them closer to eye-level. "Make me have to compare them myself."

"Depends, is it working?"

His smile grew, spreading slowly to reveal teeth, before he straightened. "Looks like. Guess I'll take a bundle. Unless you've already closed out the register?"

"You're in luck." Or maybe she was. "Did you just want the movies?" She'd offered special pricing whether people wanted any two or all three, in the hopes that that would drive up sales.

"Well, I should probably get all three—pretend I understand Shakespeare." He slid a book and a copy of each movie over to her.

"It's a comedy, without even any nonhuman creatures, so you should be okay," Mira assured, running his card. "Just remember not to read into Dogberry's lines too much."

"Noted."

Their fingers brushed when he took the bag with his purchase, which probably happened with almost every customer Mira had ever served, but absurdly, this time the bit of contact felt different, significant. Bizarrely apropos, the final line of the college kids' overly dramatic rendition of "Where Do We Go From Here?" floated toward them.

It was followed closely by, "So, drinks at my place?" and a round of agreement.

Mira hesitated a second, watching Jordan.

"Thanks," he said.

"My pleasure. Enjoy." She shot him a hopefully nonchalant smile and made her way over to the karaoke station. The college kids chimed a giddy wave of *thank you*s as they got their coats on and left the store. Mira shut off the laptop they'd been using for karaoke, then offered a "have a good rest of your night" to a couple wearing Evil League of Evil tee shirts as they made their way out.

When she came back out from putting the computer in her office, Jordan was the only other person left in the store.

"Did you want to get something else? Buffy comics, maybe?" Mira asked lamely.

"Well, I was just thinking, it's late. You probably shouldn't walk home alone, and"—he smiled—"I have a feeling we're going in the same direction."

They'd had a good time chatting the other day, when he'd come to the store, but being alone ramped up the awkwardness to its previous levels. It was a very gentlemanly offer, though. "There's still a lot to do before I can close up," she said apologetically.

"Oh, well, I could help," he offered almost predictably. "Or stay out of your way, whichever you prefer."

She couldn't figure him out, but weird as being alone with him might turn out, declining the offer seemed rude. Still, Mira felt obliged to point out, "You don't have to do that."

"I know," Jordan answered instantly, entirely unperturbed.

"Okay, thanks," she said inanely, suddenly feeling self-conscious crossing the store in front of him, dressed as a companion.

"Thanks again for hanging around," Mira said as she locked up the store.

"My pleasure. Really," Jordan assured, his breath fogging by his mouth. It hadn't even taken her long to finish up. Still, the street around them was dark and a little icy with freshly frozen puddles. Staying to walk her home had definitely been the right call.

"So, did you have a good time?" she asked, huddling in her coat, hands in her pockets.

"Yeah, I did. Thanks again for inviting me."

"Of course."

How faultlessly polite of both of them, not that Jordan had been insincere. It had definitely been a once-in-a-lifetime experience for him. He racked his brains for a way to break the awkwardness as they walked on in silence. "So people had some interesting costumes, like that guy who won," he finally said.

Mira glanced up at him for a second. "Yeah, it's tough, actually. So many of Whedon's characters are incredibly interesting, and yet their clothes tend to be somewhat mundane, because generally, they live in the real world."

"I saw this one guy, he just had a nametag that said 'God.' Was that the Whedon take on religion or something?"

"No, that was—" Her answer was cut off by a gasping cry as she slid on the icy sidewalk beside him.

Jordan reached out automatically, catching her so she didn't fall. With her pressed against him, the difference in their heights was even more obvious. He could feel the puff of her startled breath against his chest, at the opening of his coat.

"Oz," Mira said after a moment.

"As in the Wizard of?" Jordan asked without thinking.

"No, sorry. The character."

"Oh." Jordan nodded, though he still wasn't following. His brain finally caught up to their position, though, reminding him to let her go. He hesitated for a heartbeat with her watching him, then looped her arm through his to prevent further mishaps.

She looked away first, lowering her gaze to the street. They took a couple steps before she spoke again. "So Oz, he's a werewolf from *Buffy*, and a guitar player. And kind of a genius. One Halloween, in the show, his costume is a nametag that—"

"Says 'God,'" he finished with her, catching on. "That's clever." They'd reached their building, almost too soon. "What about your character, or costume?" Jordan asked, holding the door open for her. He was pretty sure there was more to it than those idiots' claims from earlier.

Mira's arm slipped out from the crook of his as she stepped inside. "Inara? She's from *Firefly*, a futuristic series that literally involves space cowboys."

"That sounds pretty cool." And pretty odd, but he didn't want to offend her. People had been intense with their adulation of all things Joss Whedon tonight, though when she spoke about the guy, Mira seemed more knowledgeable and appreciative than fanatical. When they reached her apartment, Jordan found himself wishing they lived on a higher floor.

Mira turned toward him, keys in hand. "Thanks again, for waiting for me."

"No problem." He should probably say good night, but instead, Jordan just stood there, looking at the curl of hair that had drifted forward, over her eyebrow; at her eyes, with the bit of gold around them; at the pinkness of her lips.

She was watching him too.

Jordan stepped forward, hesitated, then put his hands on her upper arms. All he could really feel was the padding of her coat sleeves, but then her chin tilted up, and her smile dropped to something more serious, and her lips parted just barely. A steadying breath later, Jordan bent to kiss her.

Four

MIRA SMILED AT THE SUNSHINE streaming through the crisp air as she stepped outside. She'd gotten plenty done in the morning hours at the store, even if her mind had all too frequently gone back to last night's kiss, but the point was she could take a couple of hours off before helping Charlie close up tonight. She should have lunch and then go to the park. Or maybe she should grab a book and have lunch in the park.

Or, she could make a couple sandwiches and see if maybe Jordan wanted to have a picnic. Their kiss last night had been sweet, and soft. And wonderful. Of course, Jordan might already have plans today, but it wasn't like there was any harm in asking, right?

It felt like it was going to be a good day, overall. Even her key sticking again only made Mira shake her head with a wry smile. She jiggled and tugged, finally getting the key to turn when the door down the hall opened.

"Oh, hey, Mira," Lisa said, coming out of the apartment with Jordan behind her. "Quiet day at the store?"

"Yeah, um, hi," Mira stammered, looking between the two as something in her chest constricted.

"Hi," Jordan said with an easy smile that stilled the air for a heartbeat.

"You know, I actually have work I need to get done, so excuse me. Sorry." Mira pushed the door to her apartment open, turning away from them. "Enjoy your afternoon," she said, slipping inside.

The click of her door shutting held an unidentifiable finality. Mira dropped her purse and keys onto a side table and blew her breath out in a steady stream, then sank to the floor.

It shouldn't have mattered, seeing him with Lisa. They'd hit it off when Mira'd introduced them, and she had seen them talking to each other at the store last night.

And either way, she had no claim to him. It wasn't as though a kiss meant anything. For most people nowadays, even sex didn't imply any sort of commitment or obligation.

Lisa simply had more in common with Jordan. Even their heights were better suited to each other's. Mira should have been happy for her friend.

But in that moment, she just couldn't be that good a person.

Bread, roast beef, maple-glazed chicken, mayo, tomatoes, pickles, mustard, cheese—Havarti and Swiss—lettuce, cucumbers. Jordan repeated the list as he made his way down the street. *Plates, napkins, plastic knives.* Had he forgotten anything? The other bag held some iced teas and a couple bottles of water.

It wasn't gourmet, but Jordan was relying on the cuteness of surprise. And well, technically, he didn't know if she was free, so this was better than just bringing a couple of sandwiches that could wind up soggy.

Inside, a low murmur surrounded him, but Mira was nowhere to be seen. Jordan crossed the store, glancing up every aisle, but he still didn't see her. He lingered by the Date a Book display, waiting for the cashier to finish ringing up a few customers.

"Can I help you?" the guy asked when Jordan approached.

"Is, well, is Mira around?"

The cashier hid his confusion almost instantly. "I'm sorry, is there a problem? I'd be happy to help you."

"No, no. I just wanted to come say hi."

"Oh." The guy nodded blankly, then the words seemed to register. "Let me go check if she's available."

"Thanks," Jordan said as much to himself as to the cashier's receding back. He shifted both bags to one hand so he could tap his fingers on the counter more comfortably. Honestly, he was getting pretty hungry. He'd had a long day at work, and the slice of maple-glazed chicken he'd tried at the deli had gotten his appetite going.

"I'm sorry," the cashier said, reappearing from between bookshelves, drawing Jordan away from their bookmark display. "She's not."

"Oh." Lisa had told him that Mira worked every night the store was open, but maybe tonight was an exception. This was the downside of surprises, apparently.

"Can I recommend something for you? Or maybe you'd like to try one of our mystery books?"

"I'm still getting through my last one, but well, thanks anyway."

The cashier offered him a tight-lipped smile, disappointed at the lack of a sale or maybe just tired of dealing with him.

"G'night," Jordan said, turning away. He'd looked forward to seeing Mira again, but apparently the evening would be spent tinkering with his latest project instead. He was really close to getting the timing down, actually, so at least there was that.

Five

Mira sighed, staring at the blocks of red in her spreadsheet, each one representing a discrepancy in their inventory counts. Some people stole—books, bookmarks, anything—there wasn't much of a way around that, but the recent increase was disturbing.

A knock on the office door preceded the squeak that signified its opening.

"Charlie, we're really going to need to talk about—" Mira cut herself off when she saw who'd opened the door.

"Brought you a mocha," Lisa said, holding out a foam cup. They hadn't spoken since running into each other last weekend, though that wasn't too out of the ordinary with Mira's work schedule.

"Thanks." Mira half-rose from her chair to take the coffee, then plopped back down as Lisa leaned back against the doorjamb with her own drink. "What's going on?" Mira asked in what was hopefully a sufficiently chipper tone.

Lisa's eyes narrowed. "Just taking a break. Thought I'd come see you."

"Oh, are you having a productive day?" Never, in all the time they'd known each other, had they had a conversation that was so unbearably stilted. Mira tilted the mocha to her mouth in a desperate attempt to restore normalcy with the kick of chocolaty coffee.

"It wasn't what you think," Lisa said, cutting straight through the hovering awkwardness.

"I don't know what you mean." Mira hadn't seen Jordan since that run-in either, which was probably a good thing. She didn't want to contemplate the potential development of his and Lisa's relationship, and not seeing him in the halls had definitely helped that. On the other hand, she needed to snap out of it and be a decent friend. "How are things going with you two?"

"Oh come on." Lisa straightened from the wall to take the two steps necessary for her long legs to cross Mira's office. "You have to know I wouldn't do that to you."

"I don't see it that way," Mira said honestly, swiveling in her chair to keep Lisa in sight as she leaned against the desk. "I don't have any kind of a claim here, and you guys seemed to get along." And if that really wasn't the case, why had Lisa been in his apartment?

"Okay, entirely rational and unemotional an approach as that is, all of us can see that you like him."

All *of them*?

"Well, except Jordan himself," Lisa clarified before Mira had a full-blown heart attack. "But for what it's worth, he definitely seems to like you too."

Mira sipped her mocha to postpone answering. "Oh, I doubt it," she said eventually. "Anyway, tell me what's been going on with you. How's the research?"

"You know, I got a little sidetracked recently, but it'll be fine." She glanced at her watch. "Actually, do you want to go take a walk? You shouldn't spend so much time in this windowless cubby."

"You know I spend most of my time out in the store itself. And it is not that bad in here." Or at least, she was usually too busy to notice how depressing the office was.

"Imagine if you were eight inches taller," Lisa teased with her trademark smile. "Come on, humor me."

"All right, okay." Mira saved the spreadsheet and stood. "But if the owner happens to have spontaneously flown in from Brazil or wherever he is nowadays, you'll have to tell him I put up much more of a fight."

"Deal," Lisa said, following her out.

Jordan glanced toward Kelsey to see if she was making any progress with the cashier. She seemed to have the young girl on board, or at the very least not objecting quite as vociferously as when they'd first come in. The store was otherwise empty, so it wasn't like they were in anyone's way at the moment.

He resettled his glasses on the bridge of his nose and squinted at the joint in front of him, then adjusted the angle.

"Oh, my goodness," he heard Mira say.

Jordan shot up, nearly bumping into the robot. Her hair was pulled back today, revealing a dangling pair of sparkling earrings.

"What in the world is this?" she asked, looking more flabbergasted than impressed.

"He's a—it's a, well." How had he forgotten all the words in the English language?

"How about you show her," Lisa suggested with an amused smile.

"Right, yeah." Jordan ran one hand through his hair, rounding his project, and flipped the power switch.

Lisa ushered Mira to a better viewing position. The robot—unimaginatively named "Jordan's Book Robot 1"—came to life, reaching to his right to pick up a used book from the stack Jordan had provided. The left arm lifted the cover, gently opening the book. Light hit the top quarter of the inside cover, and Jordan snuck a glance at Mira, whose head had tilted slightly to one side as she watched JBR1's progress. The light hit the final quarter of the right-hand page, and a delicately timed moment later, JBR1's right "thumb" flipped the page, using the friction from a hidden wheel, and the left one lifted to clamp over the new page in a precise movement. The light sequence began again. *Perfect.*

"It's…reading," Mira commented, stepping closer.

"Cool," the cashier said, joining them around the robot.

"Yeah. I thought he, well, or she, I guess, I thought this would be a good mascot, for your store," Jordan explained.

Finally, Mira made eye contact with him. "You built this for the store?"

"With Lisa's help," Jordan told her.

"I think he built it for you," Lisa said simultaneously.

"I thought, well, maybe you could focus on the idea that even a robot knows nothing can beat reading a real, physical book in your hands, like you said."

"This is amazing." Mira's gaze fell back to JBR1, watching him "read."

"He doesn't process the information or anything. I mean, it's just for show, but the stepper motor times the flip of the pages, and the cams work it so the lights show his progress down each page, so the visual is stronger, hopefully. And he'll go through as many books as you give him, picking them up and setting them aside when he's done. Oh, and the power source is rechargeable, of course, so you could just plug him right in."

"I, wow, I really don't know what to say," Mira said breathlessly through a smile.

"Start with 'thank you,'" Kelsey suggested.

"Oh, no, that's fine," Jordan started to say, but Mira cut him off.

"No, she's right, sorry. Thank you. I can't believe you built this, him."

"It was fun," Jordan said honestly. "The technology is pretty basic, compared to what's out there nowadays, but designing it and getting the timing right, that was interesting. Plus,"—he stepped toward to Mira—"I figured this might mean you don't have to spend as much time coming up with marketing ideas, so we could maybe spend some more time together?" Hopefully his smile hid the nerves behind the question.

Mira's chin ducked, and then she looked up at him through her lashes as a blush covered her cheeks. "Sounds like a plan," she said quietly, before looking back to JBR1. "What in the world should we call him?"

"Oh, just kiss him already," Lisa said, shooting them an impatient look.

"The robot?" Mira asked, quickly followed by an exhaled, "Oh." Her gaze danced around the room before finally landing back on him. Her lips twisted gently to one side.

Jordan swallowed, struggling to formulate a tactful way out for her. Then her eyebrows inched up, easing his own uncertainty. He closed the remaining distance between them, and her face tilted up in a more blatant invitation. Their lips met with a soft brush, then Mira rose on her tiptoes, balancing against his shoulder. Her lips parted, and Jordan cupped her jaw, angling for a deeper kiss.

Moments later, a not-so-subtle cough filtered into his awareness. "This is a place of business you know," Kelsey reminded, and Mira dropped back to the ground, glancing briefly toward her friends.

"There is an innocent robot present," she pointed out, holding back a smile.

"Good point." Jordan stepped back, letting his hand drop. "Think you might be free for dinner?"

"How sweet, the dating rituals of different species of geeks," Lisa said drily. "You two should be on the discovery channel."

"You're one to talk," Kelsey said.

"Definitely," Mira said quietly as her friends traded quips.

"Awesome." Her smile pulled his own lips into a stupid grin. Jordan glanced at JBR1, contently flipping through his book, then bent to kiss Mira again.

Turn the page for a look at Aria Glazki's full-length romances:

Mending Heartstrings
Tasting Temptation
Mortal Musings

Available everywhere books are sold— and your local library!

Mending Heartstrings

ARIA GLAZKI

Forging Forever, Book 1

"Kane and Elle are a great example of love and what love means. It isn't always easy, but it's so worth it. I absolutely adored the book's depth.**"**

—Jessica, The Lovely Books

"A great story of finding someone when you least expect it and not letting misunderstandings stop you from being together. A fun sweet romance to curl in a chair with and get lost in.**"**

— Books Are Love

Kane's a country singer who's tangled with too many deceitful women. He's learned his lesson: girls are for flirting and fun; emotions are for his music. But after spending a night with an earnest woman unlike any he's known, he can't force her out of his mind. So he goes in search of the woman he knows only as "Elle."

On her last night in Nashville, the staunchly pragmatic Sabella found herself in a situation more suited to a romance novel than reality. Swept away, she ignored her rigidly self-imposed rules, succumbing to the fantasy just this once. But she knows real-world relationships have nothing in common with their fictionalized portrayals. When Kane unexpectedly shows up at her Portland apartment, she must choose between the practical truths she has learned and the desire for a passionate love she has struggled to suppress.

Despite the distance, Kane's tour schedule, and their meddling friends, both are drawn to the chance for a romance neither quite believes is possible.

Tasting Temptation

ARIA GLAZKI

Forging Forever, Book 2

"*Tasting Temptation* is an enjoyable read with some very hot naughtiness thrown in... The author does a phenomenal job.**"

— Teri, Sportochick's Musings

After last summer's failed attempt at romance, Gina is absolutely done with men. And especially with millionaires. She has a good job as a fashion editor and amazing friends, and she's decided she needs nothing else. All she really misses is the sex. But that rush just isn't worth the risk of being ensnared in another relationship. When the hot bartender at her best friend's Sonoma wedding suggests some harmless stress relief, she takes him up on the offer. When it's sufficiently satisfactory, she indulges in a repeat—for the road. When she learns he's actually the wealthy owner of the vineyard, the mix of fury and fear is damped only by the knowledge that she never has to see him again.

Hunter Cavaliere is determined to honor his grandfather's legacy, and so far, he's right on track. The vineyard is thriving, he has plans for expansion, and his wines speak for themselves. The only thing missing is the right woman to share it all. But through his grandparents' marriage, Hunter learned what true love is, and he's unwilling to settle for anything else. A woman who judges him because of his money definitely isn't high up on his list. Still, when circumstance unbelievably keeps bumping him into the intriguing brunette from Portland, he can't shake the feeling that she is someone he should pursue.

Gina's poised to run the other way, but one more taste of Hunter may just prove too tempting to resist.

Mortal Musings

ARIA GLAZKI

"Allie and Brett are captivating and their chemistry is magnetic. The story is sweet, magical, and marvelously twisty.**"**

— Char, Lightning City Book Reviews

"Glazki's writing is brilliant and hooks you right in.**"**

— For the Love of Fictional Worlds

Muse Alexandra has had it with the arrogant, ungrateful humans she is obligated to inspire. When the internal ranting of her latest charge pushes her past reason, she disregards the rules and forces her own words through his fingers, and is instantly entrapped in mortal form. With no magic, no identity, and no resources, Allie has no alternative but to navigate the mortal realm, depending entirely on her reluctant host while discerning what exactly caused her transformation—and how to reverse it.

Brett doesn't have a chance to consider the words that mysteriously showed up on his screen; he's too distracted by the stunning woman who appeared in his office out of nowhere. Before his brain can catch up, Brett's uninvited guest becomes enmeshed in his everyday life. Her artless innocence gradually lessens his suspicions. Most importantly, the writer's block that's been plaguing him dissolves under the fantasies the naively beguiling Alexandra inspires.

All too soon, the forced proximity sparks a confounding awareness neither writer nor muse are able to resist.

— About Aria —

Aria Glazki's first kiss technically came from a bear cub. Though no fairytale transformation followed, she still believes magic can happen when the right people come together—if they don't get in their own way, that is. So now Aria writes heartfelt romances about relatable people overcoming real-world obstacles to build love that lasts.

Connect with Aria Online:

www.AriaGlazki.com
Newsletter: bit.ly/AriaGNewsletter
Facebook.com/Aria.Glazki
Twitter & *Instagram:* @AriaGlazki